E. GALARZA ELEMENTARY SCHOOL
1610 Bird Ave.
San Jose, CA 95125

DATE DUE

JA 19 '99		
FE 04 '00		
AP 04 '00		
DE 22 '00		
MY 21 '01		
OC 16 '01		
OC 29 '01		
AP 25 '02		
MY 03 '02		
OC 16 '02		
OC 29 '02		
OC 30 '03		
OC 22 '03		

DEMCO 38-297

Volcano!

NATURE'S DISASTERS

Volcano!

Hammer

Margaret Thomas

A LUCAS · EVANS BOOK

CRESTWOOD HOUSE
New York
Collier Macmillan Canada
Toronto
Maxwell Macmillan International Publishing Group
New York   Oxford   Singapore   Sydney

To Mom and Dad
with love and thanks

COVER: Mount St. Helens erupting in full force on May 18, 1980. Its giant cloud
    of ash rose 12 miles into the sky.
FRONTIS: After the Mount St. Helens eruption, smoke rises from inside the crater.
PAGE 7: Mount St. Helens's hollowed-out crater one year after the blast.

PHOTO CREDITS: *Cover, Frontis and all interior photos,* U.S. Geological Survey Photo
Library; *with the exception of Page 8,* Krafft/Explorer, Photo Researchers; *Page 17
(top)* NOAA; *and Page 42,* J. D. Griggs/U.S. Geological Survey.

BOOK DESIGN: Barbara DuPree Knowles   DIAGRAMS: Andrew Edwards

LIBRARY OF CONGRESS CATALOGING-IN-PUBLICATION DATA

Thomas, Margaret.
    Volcano! / by Margaret Thomas.—1st ed.
        p.   cm. — (Nature's disasters)
    SUMMARY: Examines the nature, origins and dangers of volcanoes, and discusses
the warning system that detects threatening eruptions.
    ISBN 0-89686-595-9
    1. Volcanoes—Juvenile literature.   [1. Volcanoes.]   I. Title.   II. Series.
QE521.3.T49   1991   551.2'1—dc20   90-45372

Crestwood House   Collier Macmillan Canada, Inc.
Macmillan Publishing Company   1200 Eglinton Avenue East
866 Third Avenue   Suite 200
New York, NY 10022   Don Mills, Ontario M3C 3N1
                        First Edition

Printed in the United States of America   10 9 8 7 6 5 4 3 2 1

Contents

Volcano!

I t was a quiet day in August A.D. 79. The people of Pompeii were celebrating the birth of the Roman ruler Augustus. It was also the day after the celebration and feast to honor Vulcan, the god of fire.

The farmers spent their day tending the rich fields. Grapes, olives and other crops covered the slopes of Mount Vesuvius. The people were unconcerned about living at the base of the **volcano.** They had never heard of their mountain erupting. It was said that the flat-topped mountain had a depression at the peak where Roman troops had once hidden. To the villagers it was a quiet mountain.

But on August 24, without any warning, a dark cloud erupted from the volcano. The people of Pompeii ran outside to see what threatened their city. They ran through the now-darkened streets in a storm of ash and debris. Those outside fell dead after breathing in the poisonous gases. Some people hid in cellars. Buildings collapsed under the heavy ash and crushed those inside.

A plaster mold of a Mount Vesuvius victim buried by ash in the ancient city of Pompeii.

That day 16,000 people, 80 percent of the population, died. A massive mud slide buried the neighboring town of Herculaneum under 60 feet of mud. Within three days the city of Pompeii and surrounding towns disappeared under 16 feet of ash. They would not be seen again for more than 1,600 years.

Pompeii was uncovered by archeologists in the 1700s. The shapes of ancient bodies were found in the cementlike ash. To preserve them, plaster was later poured into the "ash molds." The molds show every detail of the way the victims of Pompeii dressed. They also show the agony on their faces as they died. One woman is forever "frozen" shielding her face with her clothes. She is holding on to her jewels.

Since the destruction of Pompeii, Vesuvius has erupted violently many times. Each time the people rebuilt their city on top of the buried one. Vesuvius is considered the most active volcano in Europe. The last great eruption was in 1944. Could it happen again? Many scientists think so. The great earthquake in Italy in 1980 that killed 4,800 people could be a warning. But the half a million people who live at the base of Vesuvius do not seem to worry. They continue to farm on the fertile mountainside as their ancestors have done for centuries.

THE BIRTH OF A VOLCANO

On February 20, 1943, Dionisio Pulido tended his crops as he always did in a field near Parícutin, Mexico. Suddenly the ground rumbled beneath him. The field swelled. A fissure two feet deep split the earth. Smoke and ash, thick with the sulfur smell of rotten eggs, billowed up. The intense heat continued to widen the crack. Flames and glowing rocks shot out, burning nearby trees. As Pulido watched, a volcano was born.

By the next morning the brand-new volcano had risen 30 feet. Earthquakes from under the mountain were recorded on seismographs as far away as New York. Within a week the volcano was 450 feet high. In less than a year it was 10 miles wide. It had buried Pulido's town of Parícutin in thick, smoking ash.

The Ring of Fire

The young volcano of Parícutin is just one of a string of volcanoes called the **Ring of Fire.** They outline the entire

Parícutin in Mexico grew out of a field in 1943.

Pacific Ocean—from the southern tip of South America north to Alaska, west across the water, down along the coast of Asia and as far south as New Zealand. About 80 percent of the world's active volcanoes are found in this region.

Other chains of volcanoes are found around the world. One is in the Mediterranean belt, which stretches from southern Europe to central Asia. Others are in the Hawaiian islands, the mid-Atlantic ridge and East Africa. Volcanoes are found in groups, or chains, because of the way the earth is put together.

Plate Tectonics

Scientists believe the earth's surface, or crust, consists of **tectonic plates** that move slowly past one another. They fit together like a jigsaw puzzle. These plates of solid rock float on a thick layer of hot, molten rock. This layer is called the earth's mantle. The mantle's rock is like taffy, bendable but easily shattered.

As the tectonic, or crustal, plates move across the mantle, they separate and collide. This creates earthquakes and volcanic mountain ranges. The Ring of Fire and other volcanic chains mark where the edges of the plates meet. Volcanoes are formed primarily where plates separate or subduct.

Subduction Zones

A **subduction zone** is an area where one plate moves under another. The lower plate melts in the heat of the mantle. A well of melted rock, water and gases, called **magma,** is formed. This hot fluid pushes up through the surface as an erupting volcano. Magma that flows out of the earth is called **lava.**

Separating Plates

Where crustal plates move apart, magma wells up to fill the gap, forming a volcanic mountain range. For example, in the Atlantic Ocean, two plates shift and separate in the middle of the ocean floor. Many submerged volcanoes, called seamounts, are formed. This string of volcanoes rises up from the sea floor in the north. It crosses Iceland with a

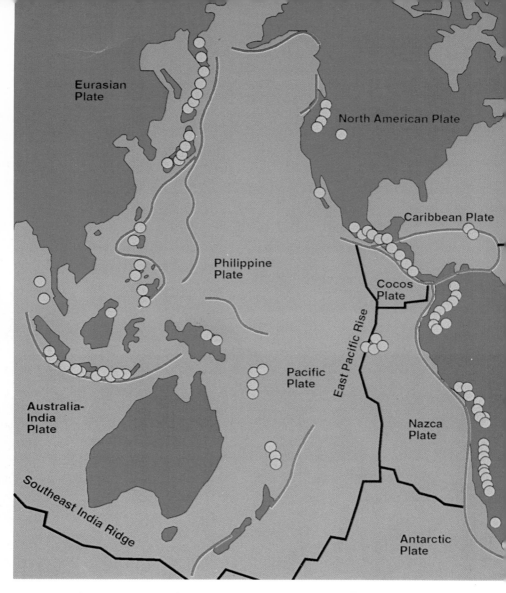

Most active volcanoes are located along the edges of the earth's tectonic plates. These are known as volcano/earthquake zones.

crack wider than an interstate highway. The magma underneath fuels Iceland's many active volcanoes.

Subduction and separation form all the volcanoes found

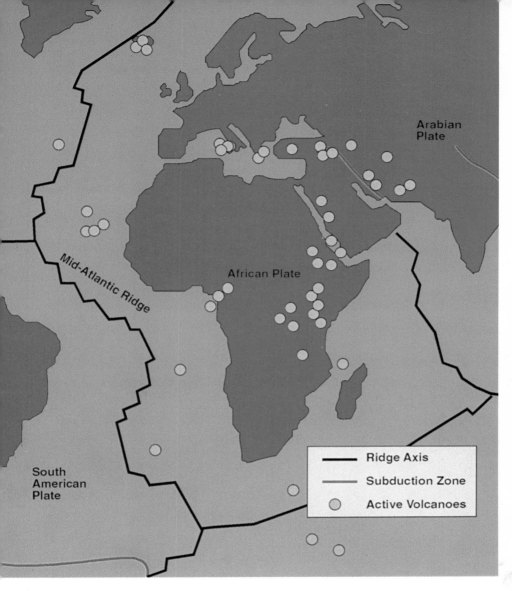

As two plates pull apart or push against each other, volcanoes are formed.

where two plates meet. But there are also volcanoes in the middle of crustal plates. The Hawaiian volcanoes are 2,000 miles from the nearest plate edge.

Hot Spots

The Hawaiian volcanoes have emerged over a large well of magma called a **hot spot.** As the plates shift, the magma melts through the crust, making individual blobs of magma. Each blob breaks through the weakened surface like a candle flame under a moving piece of paper. As the plate moves over the hot spot, a chain of volcanoes is made across the Pacific Ocean. The oldest ones are in the northwest part of the ocean and the newest in the southeast. As the plate moves a volcano away from the hot spot, the volcano stops erupting. Volcanologists (scientists who study volcanoes) believe that the island of Hawaii lies above the hot spot. It fuels the volcano Kilauea. A new underwater volcano is being built off the island's south coast. It has been named the Loihi seamount.

People rarely get to see the birth of a volcano. Most volcanoes have been here for thousands of years. Mount St. Helens in the United States erupted around 2000 B.C. It then violently blew up again in 1980.

Volcanoes have been built up, destroyed and rebuilt over the centuries. An active volcano is one that has erupted sometime in recorded history. Each of the earth's 400 to 500 of these has a unique cycle of activity and dormancy.

Dormancy is the period between eruptions, when the volcano is usually building up steam for future explosions. Studies in Iceland show that more powerful eruptions often follow long periods of dormancy.

Old volcanoes that have not been active at all in recorded history are said to be extinct. However, no one ever knows for sure. Lassen Peak in California was once considered extinct. But in 1914 it blew its top, destroying the forests around it. Now it is said to be dormant.

THE ANATOMY OF A VOLCANO

There are three basic types of volcanoes: the shield, the cinder cone and the composite. The shape of a volcano and how explosive it is are determined by the type of magma inside it. Magma contains many elements in varying amounts. The most important element is **silica.** Silica is the most common mineral in the earth's crust. It is the main ingredient in granite and sandstone. Magma with a lot of silica is very thick and sticky. Magma with only a little silica makes a very fluid lava called **basalt.**

The Shield Volcano

Thousands of thin layers of basalt lava build up the broad, gradual slopes of the **shield volcano.** The fluid lava flows

An aerial view of a shield volcano, the Kilauea caldera, in Hawaii.

quickly and travels long distances. When the lava hardens, it builds up the volcano's base rather than its height.

The five volcanoes forming the island of Hawaii are shield volcanoes. Mauna Loa's broad base measures 60 miles long and 30 miles wide. Mauna Kea is slightly larger. From its base on the ocean floor, it is 33,500 feet high. Although these volcanoes have gradual slopes, they are as tall as any mountain.

Because of its fluid basalt lava, the shield volcano is not explosive. Its lava flows from the main crater or oozes out of long cracks on the volcano's slopes. These cracks are called **fissures.** If the gas content is high, shield volcanoes can spout bright lava fountains that shoot out like Fourth of July fireworks. The Hawaiian volcano Kilauea has spit red-hot lava as high as 1,900 feet. Yet this is a weak eruption compared to Mount St. Helens's 12-mile-high ash cloud.

Cinder Cone

A **cinder cone** volcano has tall, steep sides built up by layers of cinder and ash. Its magma is high in silica rock. It explodes in fiery clouds of ash rather than flowing with lava. Cinder cones tend to be small. They are difficult to climb because of loose layers of ash. Parícutin in Mexico is a typical cinder cone volcano.

Composite Volcanoes

The most common type of volcano is the **composite.** It has layers of lava and ash that build up the curved slopes. Mount St. Helens, Mount Vesuvius and Mount Fuji in Japan are all composite volcanoes. They are some of the most explosive in the world.

Parícutin, a cinder cone volcano in Mexico.

A composite volcano located in the Cascade Mountains.

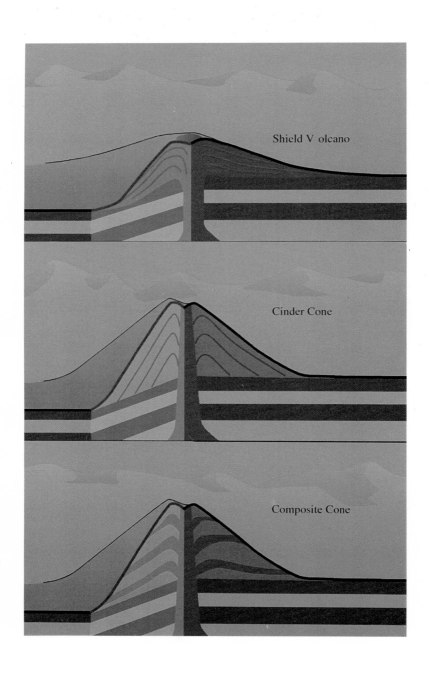

Shield Volcano

Cinder Cone

Composite Cone

18

Craters and Calderas

A **crater** is a steep-sided hole at the peak of a volcano. It is the opening to the long tube that leads down into the magma chamber. Active volcanoes may have more than one crater. They smoke and let off steam, releasing some of the pressure.

If a crater is more than a mile wide, it is called a **caldera.** It is formed when magma is exploded out. The top of the volcano collapses into itself. The largest caldera is La Garita in Mexico. It is 28 miles wide.

A plume of smoke rises from the dome that is forming inside the crater as Mount St. Helens rebuilds itself.

Crater Lake in Oregon was formed by the eruption

At one time there was a large volcano named Mount Mazama. It was 9,900 feet high. Over 6,500 years ago it blew 10 square miles of debris into the air. It left a caldera

of an ancient volcano over 6,500 years ago.

6 miles wide and almost 4,000 feet deep. Over time, water has filled in the caldera, and it is now known as Crater Lake in Oregon.

DESTRUCTIVE FIREWORKS

When you think of volcanoes, you picture fiery red lava flowing down in glowing ribbons from a bubbling crater. But volcanoes also erupt in other ways. Volcanic ash, bombs, mud slides, pyroclastic flows, and poisonous gas clouds all make volcanoes a major threat.

Lava

Lava is molten magma that erupts up from the ground. Basalt lava is thin and runny. The speed of a lava flow depends on how steep the slope is. The speed also depends on how hot the lava is, how quickly it cools and how much gas is trapped inside it. Lava can flow inches per day or race over the land at 30 miles an hour.

Cooling a lava flow to stop it from spreading into a backyard during Kilauea's 1987 eruption.

A smooth *pahoehoe* lava flow from Hawaii's Kilauea volcano.

Lava cools from the outside in. It hardens into a dark, fine-grained rock. Underneath the black, shiny surface, the flow is still moving. It crackles like a campfire as it breaks the hard surface above.

The moving lava underneath creates a pattern on the rock above. **Pahoehoe** (pah-hoy-hoy) is a term taken from the Hawaiians. It means "lava that you can walk on." Its shiny, wrinkled surface looks like coils of rope. Jagged, rough lava is called **aa** (ah-ah), which means "lava that you cannot walk on," or the pain that you feel if you do.

It takes a long time for lava to cool. Lava fields in Iceland still smoke 15 years after an eruption. The ashy surface feels cool, but if you brush the loose ash away, the ground will burn your hand.

The heat of the lava is deadly. But the flows usually move too slowly to threaten lives. One volcanologist studying Hawaiian lava sat down on a flow to eat his lunch. He thought it was solid rock but found it was still moving!

There is usually plenty of time for people to leave their homes when lava flows toward them. Houses, though, cannot escape. They are swallowed up and burned in the liquid heat. In Hawaii the still-active volcano Kilauea has been erupting off and on since 1983. By 1990 two-thirds of the houses in the surrounding area had been destroyed by lava.

Tephra

Thick, sticky magma can plug the throat of a volcano. Pressure builds up until trapped gas explodes through the magma plug. **Tephra** is the hardened magma rock that is blasted high into the air.

Tephra comes from the Greek word for volcanic ash. It can be as tiny as dust or as huge as great chunks of rock. There are two types of tephra eruptions: tephra falls and pyroclastic flows.

A tephra fall is a shower of ash. It is a thick wet paste that is thrown up into the air. Tephra is heavy and sticky. When it falls thickly to the ground, it can collapse large buildings and clog machinery. When Mount Augustine in

(OPPOSITE PAGE) A lava fountain shooting up from Kilauea, one of the most active volcanoes in the world.

Alaska erupted in 1986, it shot so much ash into the air that it made the automatic streetlights stay on for days.

A volcanic watch has been set up by the Federal Aviation Administration to warn airplanes of tephra clouds. This will prevent accidents like the one that happened to a Boeing 747 in 1989. The plane flew through an ash cloud from the Redoubt volcano in Alaska. It lost all power and fell over 13,000 feet before the pilot could restart its engines.

Most of the tephra from a volcano falls to the ground. The smaller tephra dust is carried up into the atmosphere and around the world. El Chichón in Mexico made the largest and longest-lasting tephra cloud ever observed by satellite. It rose 16 miles into the sky. The blanket of ash lasted for more than a month.

Tephra creates an invisible curtain that hangs in the sky for years. It blocks out the sun and lowers the global tem-

The tephra cloud from Mount Augustine during its 1986 eruption.

perature. The eruption of Tambora in Indonesia in 1815 created a huge ash cloud. It grew so cold that the next year was called the "year without a summer."

Bombs and Pyroclastic Flows

Bombs are larger chunks of ash and molten lava that are thrown into the sky. They become twisted and harden in the air. Magma that becomes foamy hardens into a light rock full of holes called pumice. The holes are popped bubbles where gas escaped. Rafts of pumice weighing several tons float in the ocean for years after major eruptions like those from Tambora.

Pyroclastic flows are fast floods of hot gas and rock. The poisonous gases can reach temperatures of 1,400 degrees Fahrenheit. The flood stays close to the ground. This deadly mixture can travel well over 100 miles an hour. It burns everything in its path and is impossible to escape.

The town of St. Pierre on the island of Martinique was destroyed by the eruption of Mount Pelée in 1902. The heat and gas of the pyroclastic flow stripped away everything in its path. It killed almost everyone in less than three minutes.

Lahars

A **lahar** is a volcanic mud slide. It is started by melting snow on volcanic peaks or by heavy rains during an eruption. The water mixes with tephra to form a thick, sticky mud as heavy as wet cement.

In 1985, 22,000 people were killed by a lahar. A small eruption of the volcano Nevado del Ruiz in Colombia melted

the snow. It triggered a 130-foot wall of mud that buried the entire city of Armero. Mud ten feet high surged through the city streets, carrying with it everything in its path.

VOLCANIC VICTIMS

Although volcanoes erupt frequently around the world, most do not grab people's attention. In the past there have been many volcanic disasters that have killed thousands of people. Most died later from starvation and disease. Because communication was poor and transportation was slow, rescue operations could not be made easily.

In the past 500 years, volcanoes have killed, directly or indirectly, more than 200,000 people. Half of these were killed by the eruptions of Indonesia's volcanoes Tambora and Krakatau, and Mount Pelée in the Caribbean.

Tambora erupted in 1815, killing 10,000 people in the blast. Some 82,000 later died of starvation and disease. The eruption lowered the temperature around the world.

Krakatau erupted with a blast heard 3,000 miles away. A huge chunk of its cone fell into the sea and created a giant ocean wave. The wall of water killed 36,000 people on the shores of Java and Sumatra.

Mount Pelée killed 30,000 people instantly in a flood of gas hotter than 1,300 degrees Fahrenheit. There were only two survivors.

Mount St. Helens—In Our Own Backyard

For over 100 years tourists have traveled to Mount St. Helens for its serene beauty. The snowcapped summit reflected calmly in the clear waters of Spirit Lake. But early in March 1980, geologists came to the mountain to watch its dark side. The mountain was rumbling and about to show its violent potential.

Mount St. Helens is one of 15 volcanoes that make up the Cascade mountain range. This range runs along the Pacific coast from Canada to northern California. In March the volcano started to tremble and smoke. As many as 40 earthquakes an hour were being recorded on seismographs. Skiers, campers and loggers were evacuated from the slopes.

But some people did not believe that this placid mountain could destroy itself.

Eighty-three-year-old Harry Truman refused to leave. He was the innkeeper at the Spirit Lake Lodge. He had lived there for 50 years. Truman felt that he was part of the mountain and the mountain was part of him. No volcano was going to make him leave. So with some 16 cats and stray raccoons, he settled in and waited.

The mountain began to look weary under the internal pressure. Its north face bulged 300 feet out.

On May 18, 1980, an earthquake jolted the ground. The bulge gave way in one of the biggest avalanches ever recorded. The volcano released its bottled-up pressure. The north face blew out with a force 500 times greater than that of an atomic bomb. People 200 miles away heard the blast. The avalanche raced 155 miles an hour over 24 square miles. The blast of pyroclastic debris overtook it, going 700 miles an hour. One couple camping well outside of the hazard zone felt the wind and heat instantly. The ash burned and blistered their fingers.

Those who were caught in the blast zone were buried or choked by the hot ash. Everything natural or man-made in the eight-mile radius around the volcano was gone. Over 100,000 acres of timber were stripped and laid flat like matchsticks in a heap.

Mudflows triggered by the blast traveled as fast as 90 miles an hour. They flooded the Toutle River valley, collecting trees, animals and debris in the cement-like mud.

(OPPOSITE PAGE) Timber stripped and felled by the pyroclastic blast from Mount St. Helens. Over 100,000 acres of forest were destroyed.

They jammed the Cowlitz and Columbia rivers. Harry Truman and his inn were buried. Half of Spirit Lake was filled in with bubbling mud that boiled the fish. When the flow subsided, it left a bathtub-like ring around anything left standing. At its peak the mudflow had risen 66 feet above the land.

An ash cloud rose 12 miles high. It blackened the sky and started a lightning display and severe rainstorms. The cloud spread ashes over most of the United States. In some areas it was six inches thick. The ash had to be shoveled off roofs and dug out of clogged machinery. For days it looked as if it was snowing. On the street corners children sold masks made out of coffee filters.

After nine hours of activity, the volcano finally settled down. Rescue crews went in to search for survivors, but the helicopters could not land on the loose, hot ash. After two weeks the ground was still 785 degrees Fahrenheit. Over 2,000 people were airlifted out of flooded areas, and 63 people died.

The summit had been cut down 1,313 feet, forming a bowl-shaped caldera. It looked like a barren, pitted lunar landscape, although in some places the center was still bubbling.

Mount St. Helens began almost immediately to rebuild itself. A huge lava dome has bubbled up inside the caldera and stands almost 1,000 feet high. Gradually the wildlife is coming back. Plants and trees are beginning to grow again in the ashy soil.

Mount St. Helens and the other volcanoes of the Cascade range are carefully monitored. Some show signs of erupting in the future. Mount Rainier has warm, high-altitude caves. Mount Hood has active steam vents.

Mount St. Helens's broken summit overlooks the deforested shores of Spirit Lake after the eruption.

THE VOLCANO WATCHERS

People who live near volcanoes have developed a calm attitude about their disruptive neighbors. Hawaiians sit in lawn chairs and watch casually as lava inches toward them. Some make offerings to the goddess of volcanoes, Pele, to prevent disaster. Others, like Mr. Truman, do not believe harm will come to them at all.

Icelanders think nothing of fighting the fiery giants to save their homes. In 1973 on the island of Heimaey (Hay-may), Iceland, a fissure opened up without warning.

Measuring the temperature of an *aa* lava flow in Iceland.

The crack was one mile long. A curtain of fire over 500 feet high shot up into the night. The lava seeped out like glowing liquid glass. It slowly spread toward the harbor and town.

Families evacuated to the mainland. But more than 200 men stayed to save the town. Pumping water over the flowing lava could cool it and stop its movement. Crews with hoses walked on top of the flows, wetting down the lava in a cloud of smoke. They could hear the crackle and hiss of the lava hardening beneath their feet. Ships rigged with water pumps used seawater to cool the flow. More than 19 miles of pipe and over 40 pumps were used. The men sprayed 23 million gallons of water a day over the lava.

The new volcano, Eldfell, continued to erupt and grow from March to July. But slowly the lava flow stopped. More than 350 houses had been buried, but the harbor was saved. One square mile of land was added to the island.

It was not clear if cooling the lava saved the harbor or if it was just luck. Other countries have tried with little success to control volcanoes. If a major eruption happened in a heavily populated area today, thousands could die. That is why volcanologists are trying to curb disaster by predicting future eruptions.

Volcanoes give off many warnings, such as melting snowcaps, animal and bird movement, and crater lakes drying up. But by studying the inner workings of an active volcano, earlier and more efficient detection methods can be found.

Many new techniques are being developed to tap into the plumbing of a volcano and reveal its secrets. The most common detection instruments used today are tiltmeters and seismographs. More experimental methods include

The volcano Eldfell erupts on the outskirts of Heimaey, Iceland, in 1973 (ABOVE). A two-story house and a telephone pole poke through the ash that buried the town (BELOW).

laser and gravity measurements. With each new piece of equipment, new information is discovered. But more questions are raised.

Tiltmeters

Before an eruption, pressure builds up and magma pushes its way to the surface. The ground swells and bulges under the strain. The **tiltmeter** was developed by the Hawaiian Volcano Observatory to measure the ground swell. It has two containers that are connected by a tube with fluid in each side. The mechanism is placed in the ground. As the ground swells, the fluid flows from one container to another. Tiltmeters are so sensitive they can detect a change in angle of less than one microradian (.00006 degree). This change would be like putting a nickel under one end of a one-mile-long board.

Seismograph

A **seismograph** measures and records the vibrations in the earth. The movement of magma under the earth causes tremors and earthquakes. Before an eruption they tend to get more frequent and more violent.

In 1959 Kilauea's December eruption was detected six months in advance thanks to the seismograph. The tremors rose closer and closer to the surface at a fairly predictable rate. Seismologists could tell when the volcano would erupt.

The Hawaiian chain has some of the most thoroughly monitored volcanoes in the world. On Kilauea alone more than 90 tiltmeters and 50 seismographs are at work.

A survey crew measures the ground swell of a Hawaiian volcano.

The monitoring devices allow volcanologists to understand the unique characteristics of each volcano. Volcanologists can then consider any unusual tremor, gas emission or swelling as a warning sign that the volcano is active and possibly dangerous.

Because of close monitoring, there have been successful predictions. In 1983 the tiny Indonesian island of Colo had tremors and earthquakes for ten days. On July 18 there was a small eruption. Because of the volcano's past performances, 7,000 people were evacuated on July 22. The next day the volcano (called Colo) blew its top and destroyed all the homes, crops and plantations on the island, but no lives were lost.

THE GOOD VOLCANO

For all of their destruction, we could not survive without volcanoes. They are part of earth's intricate **ecosystem.** They support plant and animal life by supplying the atmosphere with carbon dioxide and water vapor.

Ash and lava flows bury and burn the land. But over time they help to fertilize the soil and create some of the most productive farmlands. On the slopes of Vesuvius the soil is so fertile farmers often have two or three harvests a year.

In tropical regions volcanic ash improves the moisture-holding capacity of the soil. With enough rainfall, areas buried by thin layers of new lava can see new plant growth in less than one year.

Even on the cold island of Iceland, farmers can grow year-round supplies of fresh fruits and vegetables. They do it by tapping into the earth's heat for **geothermal** energy.

New growth in the barren landscape of Mount St. Helens.

Since the eruption of Eldfell in 1973, the town of Vest-mannaeyjar has used the massive, black lava flows to heat homes, schools and greenhouses. Pipes are placed under the still-hot lava rock. Water is pumped through, heated and then piped out to the town. There is enough geothermal energy to supply the whole town with heat for at least another 50 years.

The 80,000 people of Reykjavik (the capital of Iceland) get their hot water from lava flows ten miles away. The water is still 200 degrees Fahrenheit by the time it reaches the city.

Recently, the volcanic energy of Hawaii's Kilauea has been tapped. A geothermal power plant was built on one of its rift zones.

At the plant, engineers drill down into the earth to collect steam that has been produced by the magma. The steam is pumped up into turbines to generate electricity. Engineers can create more steam by pumping cold water down into the hot rock. The heat turns the water to steam, which is then pumped up to turn huge turbines.

Even in simpler, more remote places, volcanic steam is used. On the small island of Paluweh in Indonesia people use geothermal energy to produce fresh water. Stalks of

An aerial view of a geothermal power plant on Hawaii's Kilauea.

hollow bamboo are placed into smoking holes in the ground. Steam collects in them. The steam is then condensed to make 100 gallons of fresh water a day.

Volcanoes can also be a good source of minerals. In Indonesia sulfur is extracted as it coats the ground around active vents. Diamonds are mined from ancient volcanoes in South Africa. A pyroclastic deposit called **pozzolana** is used to make a valuable cement that sets underwater. The ash and lava that devastate cities are used to pave roads and airplane runways. Even Lava soap uses pumice, the volcanic rock, for a scrubbing agent.

For centuries volcanoes have attracted tourists. Some people enjoy the hiking and skiing on the snow-covered slopes; others go to see the volcanoes in action. Hawaii's Volcanoes National Park is famous for allowing people within feet of smoking craters and fiery fissures. Even Mount St. Helens, which used to be a favorite camping area, now attracts millions of tourists who want to see what happened.

So far, most large eruptions have been in remote areas. As the world's population grows, more and more people are finding themselves living near volcanoes. Millions of people live under the constant threat of an eruption. It is not easy to contend with the earth's inner forces. People are learning to predict when a volcano might burst. This is our best chance to keep any more disasters from happening.

Some Famous

A.D. 79 Mount Vesuvius, Italy: 16,000 people die as the cities of Pompeii and Herculaneum are buried.

260 Ilopango, El Salvador: Eruption destroys pre-Mayan civilization.

1669 Mount Etna, Italy: 20,000 people are killed by lava and pyroclastic blast.

1783 Laki, Iceland: 10,000 people die from lava flows and starvation.

1792 Unsen, Japan: 14,000 people die from collapse of cone and by ocean waves.

1815 Tambora, Indonesia: More than 90,000 people die of famine because of severe climatic effects.

1877 Cotopaxi, Ecuador: 1,000 are killed in eruption. The highest continuously active volcano.

1883 Krakatau, Indonesia: 36,000 people are killed by ocean waves.

1902 Mount Pelée, Martinique: 30,000 people die within minutes from pyroclastic blast.

1912 Katmai, Alaska: Heavy ash deposits are one foot thick. The Valley of Ten Thousand Smokes is formed.

Volcanic Eruptions

1949   Parícutin, Mexico: 1,000 people die in the eruption of this volcano formed in 1943.

1951   Mount Lamington, New Guinea: 3,000 people are killed by pyroclastic blast.

1963   Surtsey, Iceland: A 426-foot-long island forms overnight.

1965   Taal, Philippines: 350 people die in the blast, which triggers an ocean wave on Lake Taal.

1973   Eldfell, Iceland: 350 homes are buried by lava, and water is used to cool the flows.

1980   Mount St. Helens, Washington State, U.S.: 63 people die from blast, and 100 square miles are stripped bare of foliage.

1982   El Chichón, Mexico: 187 people die, and 60,000 are left homeless.

1984   Mauna Loa, Hawaii, U.S.: Erupts with Kilauea at same time. Lava covers more than 18 square miles.

1985   Nevado del Ruiz, Colombia: 22,000 people die in mud slides.

1990   Kilauea, Hawaii, U.S.: More than two-thirds of the homes of Kalapana Gardens have been destroyed in eruptions since 1983.

Glossary

aa Lava that has a jagged, rough surface.

basalt A type of hardened lava that has little silica content, flows easily and is not explosive.

bomb A large lump of thick lava that is thrown into the air and hardens before it hits the ground.

caldera A crater larger than one mile wide, formed by the collapse of the cone after an eruption.

cinder cone A type of volcano that is built up by layers of loose ash. It tends to be very explosive.

composite volcano A type of volcano that is built up by alternating layers of lava and ash. It erupts with both pyroclastic material and lava.

crater A steep-sided depression at the summit of a volcano.

ecosystem All living and nonliving things working together to keep the environment balanced.

fissure A crack in the earth through which volcanic material erupts.

geothermal Internal heat of the earth.

hot spot A large well of magma, which breaks through the middle of a crustal plate. The Hawaiian islands are formed over a hot spot.

lahar The Indonesian term for a mud slide started by a volcanic eruption.

lava Magma that breaks through to the surface of the earth.

magma A combination of molten rock, gases and water.

pahoehoe Lava that has a shiny, wrinkly appearance.

plate tectonics The theory that the earth is made of large plates that drift over the mantle. When they separate or collide, they create earthquakes, mountain ranges and volcanoes.

pozzolana A pyroclastic deposit that forms cement underwater.

pyroclastic flows Fast floods of hot gas and rocks ejected explosively from a volcano.

Ring of Fire The earthquake and volcano belt in countries that rim the Pacific Ocean.

seismograph A monitoring device that measures ground movement.

shield volcano A large, gently sloping volcano built up by thin lava flows.

silica The main ingredient in the earth's crust. It determines how explosive magma is.

subduction zone The area where two crustal plates meet, forcing one below the other.

tectonic plates The large plates of solid rock which fit together and float over the earth's mantle.

tephra Volcanic ash.

tiltmeter A monitoring device that measures ground swell.

volcano An opening in the earth's surface where hot lava, rock and gases are forced out. A volcanic mountain is formed as the lava and rock build up around the opening.

For Further Reading

Aylesworth, Thomas G., and Virginia L. *The Mount St. Helens Disaster: What We've Learned*. New York: Franklin Watts, 1983.

Erickson, Jon. *Volcanoes and Earthquakes*. Blue Ridge Summit: PA: Tab Books, 1988.

Fodor, R. V. *Earth Afire! Volcanoes and Their Activity*. New York: William Morrow and Company, 1981.

Gilbreath, Alice. *Ring of Fire and the Hawaiian Islands and Iceland*. Minneapolis: Dillon Press, 1986.

Lauber, Patricia. *Volcano, the Eruption and Healing of Mount St. Helens*. New York: Bradbury Press, 1986.

Scherman, Katharine. *Daughter of Fire: A Portrait of Iceland*. Boston: Little, Brown, 1976.

INDEX